Feb 2020

Major League SOCCER

D.C. United

Marty Gitlin

Mitchell Lane
PUBLISHERS

2001 SW 31st Avenue
Hallandale, FL 33009

www.mitchelllane.com

Copyright © 2019 by Mitchell Lane Publishers. All rights reserved. No part of this book may be reproduced without written permission from the publisher. Printed and bound in the United States of America.

Printing   1   2   3   4   5   6   7   8

Designer: Ed Morgan
Editor: Sharon F. Doorasamy

Library of Congress Cataloging-in-Publication Data

Names: Gitlin, Marty, author.
Title: D.C. United / by Marty Gitlin.
Description: Hallandale, Florida : Mitchell Lane Publishers, [2019] | Series: Major League Soccer | Includes webography. | Includes bibliographical references and index.
Identifiers: LCCN 2018003252| ISBN 9781680202465 (library bound) | ISBN 9781680202472 (eBook)
Subjects: LCSH: D.C. United (Soccer team) | Soccer teams—United States—History.
Classification: LCC GV943.6.D32 G57 2018 | DDC 796.334/6309753—dc23
LC record available at https://lccn.loc.gov/2018003252

PHOTO CREDITS: Design Elements, freepik.com, Cover Photo: Tony Quinn/Icon Sportswire via Getty Images, p. 5 Art Bromage CC-BY-2.0, p. 6 freepik.com, p. 9 Stephen Dunn/Getty Images, p. 10 George Bridges/MCT/MCT via Getty Images, p. 11 TIM SLOAN/AFP/Getty Images, p. 12 Patrick McDermott/Getty Images, p. 15 freepik.com, p. 16 Tony Quinn/Icon Sportswire via Getty Images, p. 19 Tony Quinn/MLS via Getty Images, p. 21 Doug Pensinger /Allsport, p. 22 Stephen Dunn/Getty Images, p. 25–26 freepik.com

Contents

Chapter One
All About Major League Soccer 4

Chapter Two
Planting the Seeds of Success 8

Chapter Three
How the Game is Played 14

Chapter Four
Best of the Best 18

Chapter Five
A New World 24

What You Should Know 28
Quick Stats 28
Timeline 29
Glossary 30
Further Reading 31
On the Internet 31
Index 32
About the Author 32

Words in **bold** throughout can be found in the Glossary.

All About Major League Soccer

CHAPTER ONE

Soccer has not always been loved by sports fans in the United States. Americans love baseball, football, and basketball. But soccer is the most popular game on the planet. More than 265 million people play soccer in more than 200 countries. In most of the 200 countries, it is called football.

Americans' love of soccer began to grow in the 1990s. More kids started playing the game. Moms embraced the sport for both their sons and daughters. Television viewership of soccer climbed. Then the United States won a chance to host the 1994 FIFA World Cup. It was a first for the United States.

FIFA stands for Fédération Internationale de Football Association. It governs international soccer. As a condition of winning the FIFA bid, the United States agreed to create a professional soccer league. This league became known as Major League Soccer (MLS).

MLS kicked off with 10 **franchises** in 1996. It started small. Cities such as Chicago did not have a team that year. But an average of 17,406 fans attended MLS games in its first season. Average **attendance** continued to soar. It jumped by nearly 5,000 between 2010 and 2015. It peaked at 21,692 in 2016. The Seattle Sounders drew more than 40,000 fans per home game for five straight years.

Seattle Sounders fans show their team support during a home game with the New England Revolution at Qwest Field, in Seattle, Washington. Qwest is now known as CenturyLink Field.

Chapter One

A total of 22 teams competed in MLS in 2017. Nineteen of the 22 are based in the United States. Three are in Canada, in the cities of Montreal, Toronto, and Vancouver. The teams are divided into an Eastern Conference and Western Conference.

Major League Soccer is the most **diverse** league in the United States. A study in 2015 showed that nearly half of all MLS players were born outside of the United States and Canada. The study also revealed how popular soccer had become in the United States. It found that the United States produced more MLS players than any other country. California had 57 athletes, more than any state. Texas was second with 27.

Those players have little time to rest between seasons. The MLS schedule runs longer than any major American sport. Each team plays 34 matches—17 at home and 17 on the road. But the teams often compete only once a week. That is why their seasons last more than seven months.

All About Major League Soccer

Major Soccer League teams earn three points for a win. They receive one point for a tie. The six teams with the most points in each conference make the **playoffs**. More than half of all MLS teams move on after the regular season. But the top two in both conferences are given a **bye** in the first round. They advance while the others play one match to stay alive.

The next two rounds are two-match playoffs. The teams that score the most goals in those matches survive to compete for the **MLS Cup** title in December. Their seasons last nine months. But it is worth it for their players. They get a chance to compete for the Cup. Among the teams that have won it all is D.C. United. The franchise, which is based in the U.S. capital of Washington, D.C., is one of the MLS original members. It has a rich history.

Fun Facts

1. Major League Soccer teams travel great distances to many of their matches. Those in the Northwest spend the most time in airplanes. The Portland Timbers and Seattle Sounders flew more than 40,000 miles in 2016.

2. Soccer is the lowest scoring of all major American sports. It is rare when a team tallies more than three goals in a match. But that happened in a MLS Cup finals in 2003. San Jose scored four goals that year to defeat Chicago.

Planting the Seeds of Success

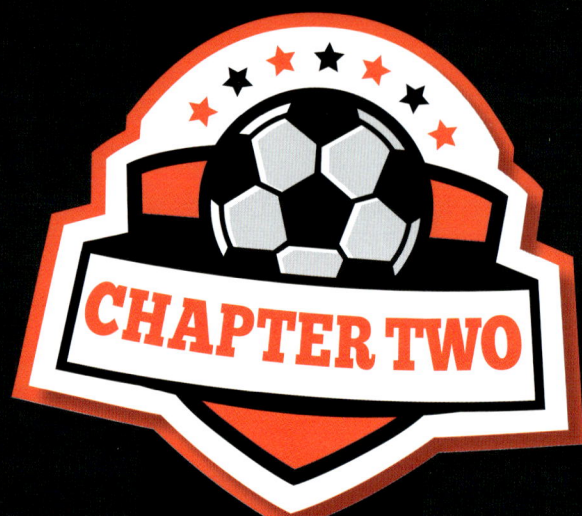

CHAPTER TWO

The date was April 6, 1996. The place was Spartan Stadium in San Jose, California. Three years of planning had finally wrapped up. Major League Soccer was set to kick into action.

Two teams graced the field that day. One was the San Jose Clash. The other was D.C. United. Nearly 32,000 fans eagerly awaited the battle. The players were nervous. It showed. Neither team performed well.

San Jose won that warm afternoon. D.C. United had started the season with a terrible 2-7 record. But the team gained **momentum**. They earned a playoff spot that season. And soon they won the first MLS title. A victory over the L.A. Galaxy clinched the **championship**.

Victor Mella (*left*) of the San Jose Clash battles with Raul Diaz Arce of D.C. United for the ball at Spartan Stadium in San Jose, California, in April 1996.

Chapter Two

San Jose's Ian Russell, (*right*), and D.C. United's Earnie Stewart battle for the ball at a game in April 2004.

D.C. United was not done dominating. They took their **momentum** and ran with it. United was the best in the league in its early years. They captured three of the first four titles and another in 2004. They won or placed second in their conference eight times in their first 12 seasons.

Great players helped D.C. United stay strong through 2007. But then the team fell on hard times. They posted a losing record every year from 2008 to 2011. They bottomed out in 2013 by winning just three matches. They scored only 22 goals and allowed 59 that year. But they recovered to earn a playoff spot every season from 2014 to 2016.

Planting the Seeds of Success

D.C. United has been the most awarded MLS franchise. Their success has gone beyond the four MLS titles. Their trophy case is filled. The team won its first U.S. Open Cup in 1996 by defeating United Soccer League rival Rochester. It won the same event in 2008 and 2013.

Perhaps the greatest victory ever for D.C. United was achieved in 1998. That is when they shut out Brazil's CR Vasco da Gama to win the InterAmerican Cup.

Vasco da Gama's Gian (*left*) receives a cleat to the head from D.C. United's Ben Olsen during the Interamerican Cup match in November 1998, at Robert F. Kennedy (RFK) Stadium in Washington, D.C.

Chapter Two

Attendance at home games has risen and fallen based on performance. D.C. United averaged more than 17,000 fans between 1996 and 2010. That was among the higher figures in the league. But it dropped to under 15,000 per game between 2011 and 2014. The team drew an average of 17,081 fans in 2016. It was an improvement. But it ranked only 17th among 20 MLS teams.

D.C. United is the only MLS franchise with a nickname that reflects team colors. They are known as the Black-and-Red. They often wear both black shorts and tops. Their road uniforms have been mostly white with some black or red. They have also worn red shorts in game action.

Paul Arriola (*left*) wears the usual black and red uniform while battling Alex Muyl of the New York Red Bulls at RFK Stadium on October 22, 2017.

Planting the Seeds of Success

That game action at home has been played at Robert F. Kennedy (RFK) Stadium. The venue was also the longtime home of the Major League Baseball and National Football League teams in Washington, D.C.

D.C. United will move to a new park in 2018. That is when Audi Field will open. It will hold about 20,000 fans. The seats will match the team colors. They will be red, gray, or black.

Hundreds of players at all positions have worn the uniforms. The talent on the field has made the Black-and-Red a success. But there is more to D.C. United than great soccer players.

Fun Facts

1 Billionaire investor George Soros was D.C. United's original owner. The Hungarian-American remained the team's owner for several years after the league began in 1996. He has also owned part of Manchester United of England. It is one of the most famous soccer teams in the world.

2 The name of the MLS Most Valuable Player award has changed twice. It was the Honda MLS Most Valuable Player award from 1996 to 2007. It was the Volkswagen MLS Most Valuable Player award from 2007 to 2014. But it was renamed the Landon Donovan Award in 2015. Donovan played for 14 seasons and won the MVP in 2009.

How the Game is Played

CHAPTER THREE

Imagine you are a goalkeeper in Major League Soccer. You are nervous and alone at the net. The team is depending on you to stop booted balls from landing in the net. You know that one goal can mean defeat. After all, many MLS matches end in a 1–0 score. But you get plenty of help from defenders. Their job is to prevent shots on goal. They try to steal the ball or kick it away from opponents.

The three midfielders and two wingbacks are the first line of defense. The midfielders play around midfield. The wingbacks play close to the center line. But they roam around the sidelines.

The goalkeeper has four other defenders closer to him. They are the fullbacks and center-backs. The two fullbacks also defend near the sidelines. The two center-backs play the middle.

Everyone else on the field has at least some offensive tasks. Two center midfielders play both offense and defense. The attacking midfielder tries to control and pass the ball to set up scores.

Wings and forwards play closest to the goal. They seek to boot the ball into the net. They sometimes slam the ball off their heads past goalkeepers. Those shots are called headers.

The forwards grab the spotlight because they score the most goals. But every player on the field is vital to success.

Goalkeeper (GK)
Right back defender (RB)
Left back defender (LB)
Center back defender (CB)
Left midfielder (LM)
Center midfielder (CM)
Right midfielder (RM)
Left forward (LF)
Right forward (RF)

Chapter Three

The teams with the best talent win games and championships. They also create **rivalries** against other top teams. Major League Soccer boasts many heated rivalries. Some are based on great playoff matches in the past. Other teams become rivals because their cities are located nearby.

Perhaps the most intense MLS rivalry is between Seattle and Portland. Both teams reside in the Pacific Northwest of the United States. Seattle has also developed a rivalry against Los Angeles. The Galaxy holds the record for most league titles with five. But the Sounders earned the crown in 2016.

Other MLS rivalries are based on long histories. Among the longest is D.C. United against New York. They have been Eastern Conference rivals since the MLS began in 1996.

Rivalries attract fans to matches. Such fan support often helps players perform well. D.C. United owned a better record at home every year from 2011 to 2016. They won 46 matches and lost only 20 at home during that time. But they won only 17 of 85 on the road.

Among those leading the cheers at D.C. United matches is Talon. He is the team mascot. He dresses in a huge bird costume. His yellow beak and black uniform make him a colorful character. Talon keeps the fans entertained with his antics.

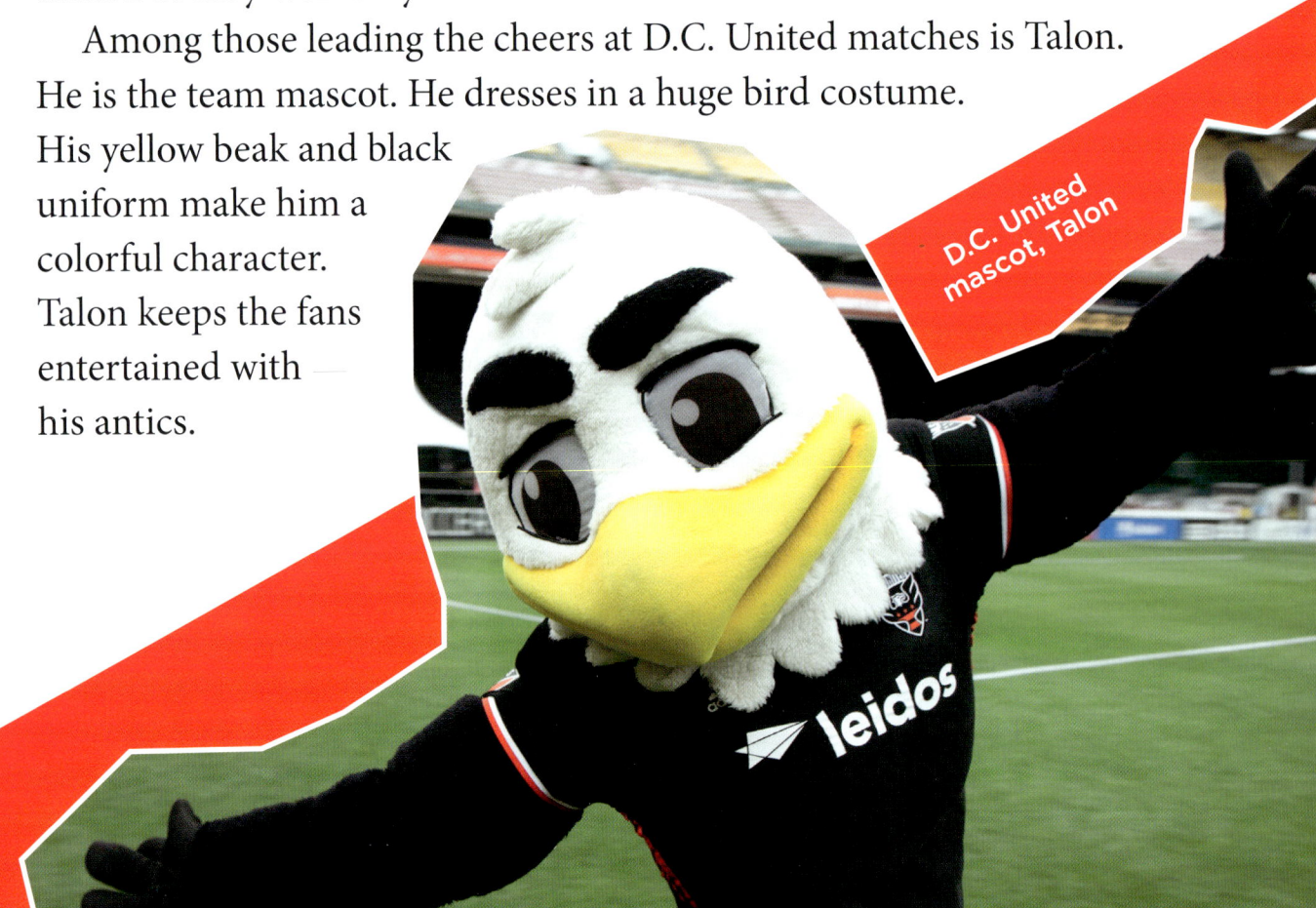

D.C. United mascot, Talon

How the Game is Played

Major Soccer League players find it hard to perform their best away from home. Long plane travel and living out of hotels can sap energy. Cheering fans bring energy to their opponents. Even teams with limited talent often win their home games.

Home fans have certainly helped D.C. United win matches. But the Black-and-Red have also had great players. They have been known for their explosive offense. They outscored all their conference rivals every year from 1997 to 1999. The 74 goals they tallied in 1998 remains an Eastern Conference record.

D.C. United last won the MLS Cup crown in 2004. They have not played for the championship ever since. The team and its fans hope that playoff berths every season from 2014 to 2016 signal a return to greatness. That greatness has been defined by some of the finest players in MLS history.

Fun Facts

1. D.C. United changed its logo in 2015. The black eagle that had been in its center since 1996 remained. But the old logo featured a soccer ball within a gold star. The team removed the soccer ball in the logo and replaced it with three small red stars.

2. The 2010 D.C. United team scored just 21 goals all season. That marks the lowest total in MLS history. The Black-and-Red were shut out in 17 of 30 matches. It is no wonder that they rarely won that year. They finished last in the Eastern Conference.

Best of the Best

CHAPTER FOUR

The first Major League Soccer championship was on the line. It was October 20, 1996. The showdown between D.C. United and L.A. Galaxy was tied at 2–2. Someone had to be a hero.

That someone was Black-and-Red standout Eddie Pope. He slammed the ball off his head. Galaxy goalkeeper Jorge Campos had no chance. The ball whizzed past him into the net.

D.C. United had captured the crown. Pope ran downfield and slid headfirst to the ground. His teammates piled on top of him. The celebration had begun. There would be much more to celebrate in the future.

The Black-and-Red can claim many stars. After all, only one team in MLS history has featured four Most Valuable Player award winners. That team is D.C. United. Marco Etcheverry (1998), Christian Gomez (2006), Luciano Emilio (2007), and Dwayne De Rosario (2011) all earned the highest individual award in Major League Soccer.

Yet one could argue that none of them were the best player in team history. Some believe Jaime Moreno tops the list.

Moreno was born in the South American country of Bolivia. He is one of the leading career MLS scorers with 133 goals. He landed on five all-MLS teams. He ranks fourth in league history with 12 playoff goals and 340 games played. Moreno played all but one season with D.C. United from 1996 to 2010.

Jaime Moreno during a match against the Seattle Sounders in 2009

Chapter Four

The star forward scored nearly three times more goals than any other player in team history. Moreno did not win a league MVP. But he did capture a Golden Boot in 1997. That honor is given to the leading scorer in the league every year. Emilio (2007) and De Rosario (2014) also won it. De Rosario is perhaps the greatest MLS player ever from Canada.

Black-and-Red stars have not only been scorers. They have also stopped great scorers from scoring. Americans Tony Perkins (2006) and Bill Hamid (2014) earned MLS Goalkeeper of the Year honors.

Perkins received plenty of help in 2006 from Bobby Boswell. Boswell was named Defender of the Year. D.C. United's Pope also won that award in 1997.

The best talent has shined in the biggest moments. But so have many other excellent D.C. United players. The top forwards have scored huge goals in MLS Cup matches. The greatest goaltenders have made big saves. The finest defenders have shut down opposing offenses.

Among the heroes were Tony Sannah and Shawn Medved. They scored goals to set up the game-winner by Pope in 1996.

More stars shined two years later in the Champions' Cup. None shined brighter than goaltender Scott Garlick. He shut out Tulsa in the finals to give D.C. United the title. The **tournament** also featured Black-and-Red forward Roy Lassiter. He scored six goals to lead all teams. That earned him the Most Valuable Player award in that event.

Best of the Best

Scott Garlick kicks the ball during a game against the Tampa Bay Mutiny at RFK Stadium in Washington, D.C.

Chapter Four

The Black-and-Red were not done tormenting the Galaxy. They beat Los Angeles to take the MLS Cup again in 1999. D.C. United midfielder Ben Olsen scored a goal and played great defense in the shutout. It was no wonder he was named Most Valuable Player in that match.

D.C. United won its fourth MLS Cup in nine years in 2004. It would not have been possible without forward Alecko Eskandarian. He was the first pick by the Black-and-Red in the 2003 **draft**. The team proved itself wise when he scored two goals to key the finals win over Kansas City.

Alecko Eskandarian heads the ball against the Kansas City Wizards during the MLS Cup on November 14, 2004.

Best of the Best

Another hero emerged for D.C. United in 2013. That is when midfielder Lewis Neal scored the lone goal in the Open Cup championship. Hamid shut out MLS rival Real Salt Lake in that match.

Every player that has worn the Black-and-Red is part of their history. They have all helped make D.C. United one of the greatest franchises in Major League Soccer.

Fun Facts

1. D.C. United has won the MLS Supporters' Shield four times. The award is given to the team that racks up the highest point total every season. The Black-and-Red won it in 1997, 1999, 2006, and 2007.

2. D.C. United star Dwayne De Rosario had a match to remember in 2008. He played for the MLS All-Stars against British team West Ham United. It was held in his hometown of Toronto, Canada. He scored the winning goal in a 3–2 victory.

3. There would be no more MLS titles for D.C. United after 2004. But there were U.S. Open Cup championships in 2008 and 2013. The star in the first of those two was Brazilian Helbert Frederico Carreiro da Silva, known simply as Fred. His goal clinched the 2008 title.

A New World

CHAPTER FIVE

They came from Mexico, Argentina, Germany, Nigeria, and Brazil. Talent from all over the world graced the D.C. United roster in 2017.

They stream in to play for other MLS teams as well. They arrive from Europe, South America, and Africa. They love that they play an **international** sport.

Some of those who compete in Major League Soccer do not speak English. They have never performed in the United States. They have never visited American cities. They must adjust. It is not easy.

Each MLS team can carry a roster of 30 players. Only eight can be international. Many of the international players travel thousands of miles from their home countries. For many, American life is challenging, with its different customs, food, and language. Daily life is often much harder than kicking a ball into a net.

It is also sometimes difficult for international players to live away from their families. They must find a new home. They must learn how to buy things with US money. They are in a world of strangers. They try to make friends. They are welcomed by new teammates and coaches, but they cannot always understand them.

Their one comfort zone should be the soccer field. But even playing a familiar sport is harder. International players do not always know what teammates are saying on the field. They need help to understand commands of their coaches. They cannot answer questions from the media without an **interpreter**.

Chapter Five

Travel in the United States and Canada can also be tough. They are two of the largest countries in the world. International players most often come from much smaller nations. They are used to traveling short distances to matches on buses or trains. They must get used to spending hours on planes and sleeping in hotels.

Major League Soccer teams often play on Saturday nights. But they leave on Thursday or Friday. Matches end late. Players do not return home until Sunday. They often spend four days on the road. That can be easy for American and Canadian players who speak English. It can be brutal for those who do not know the language.

Even the weather can be harsh on international players. The weather within smaller countries is often nearly the same. MLS players might have a Wednesday match on a cool evening in Canada. Three days later they could play in the scorching heat of Texas. Then a week later they might play in the heavy rains of Portland.

A New World

The change on the field goes beyond calling the sport soccer instead of football. Foreign players must **adapt** to a different style. Major League Soccer boasts a faster pace than the sport in other parts of the world. But the best athletes excel in MLS. The greatest players in D.C. United history are prime examples. Etcheverry arrived from Bolivia. Gomez played in Argentina before wearing the Black-and-Red. Emilio had been a standout in Brazil. They all became MLS superstars.

Not every D.C. United player emerged as a star. But they all proudly wore the uniform of a great franchise.

Fun Facts

1. In 2017, the MLS began to require that each team reserve two spots for homegrown players. Those are players groomed in the team's youth soccer program. D.C. United had been using homegrown players for many years. Their homegrown players have led the league in minutes on the field since 2008.

2. The most famous international player to join an MLS team was David Beckham. He starred in England and Spain before signing a huge contract to play for the Los Angeles Galaxy. Beckham helped his team win the MLS Cup in 2011 and 2012.

What You Should Know

- D.C. United is one of five originally named MLS teams. The others are the Columbus Crew, New England Revolution, Los Angeles Galaxy, and Colorado Rapids.
- Bruce Arena coached D.C. United to two of its first three championships. He went on to coach the U.S.'s men's national soccer team.
- Talon has been the D.C. United mascot since the first year of the team in 1996.
- Top MLS goalkeeper Bill Hamid still played for the Black-and-Red in 2017. He started with D.C. United as a homegrown player in 2010.
- D.C. United won the MLS Supporters' Cup for scoring the most points four times. But they only won the title in two of those years. They took both crowns in 1997 and 1999.
- Ben Olsen remained with D.C. United after retiring as a player. He became head coach in 2010. Olsen was still in that position in 2017.
- Thomas Rongen coached the Black-and-Red to the MLS title in 1999. The team struggled the next two seasons. He was replaced in 2002.
- D.C. United won four MLS titles in its first nine seasons. The only other team that won more than one during that time was San Jose.
- Only two MLS players scored more career goals than D.C. United star Jaime Moreno. They are Landon Donovan of the Galaxy and Jeff Cunningham. Cunningham played for many different teams.
- D.C. United has never lost an MLS Cup. They played for the championship four times and won them all. But they have not played for one since 2004.
- The Black-and-Red are based in Washington, D.C. They have many fans in nearby states Virginia and Maryland.
- D.C. United shares Robert Kennedy Stadium with the baseball Nationals. But they will not have to share their home park when Audi Field opens in 2018.

Quick Stats

1996	Wins MLS Cup, U.S. Open Cup
1997	Wins MLS Cup, Supporters' Shield
1999	Wins MLS Cup, Supporters' Shield, U.S. Open Cup
2004	Wins MLS Cup
2006–2007	Wins Supporters' Shield
2008	Wins U.S. Open Cup
2013	Wins U.S. Open Cup

D.C. United Timeline

1996
D.C. United plays its first MLS regular season game, losing to San Jose, 1–0; Black-and-Red defeats Los Angeles in MLS Cup to win first league title; a 3–0 victory over Rochester gives D.C. United its first U.S. Open championship.

1997
D.C. United defeats Colorado to capture second straight MLS crown.

1998
Win over Club de Regatas Vasco da Gama gives D.C. United InterAmerican Cup title.

1999
Black-and-Red beat Los Angeles for third MLS championship.

2004
Defeat of Kansas City in MLS Cup gives D.C. United fourth league title.

2008
D.C. United wins U.S. Open Cup with win over Charleston of the United Soccer League.

2013
A 1–0 win over MLS rival Real Salt Lake gives Black-and-Red a second U.S. Open crown.

2016
D.C. United falls to Montreal in the first round of third straight playoff appearance.

Glossary

adapt
To change in order to fit a new situation

attendance
The number of people at an event

bye
Earning the right not to play a round in the playoffs

championship
One or more contests held to decide the winner, or champion

diverse
Not the same; different

draft
The choosing of high school or college players by sports teams

franchise
A sports organization that features a team

international
Having to do with two or more countries

interpreter
A person who takes something that has been said in one language and repeats it in another

MLS Cup
The championship match in Major League Soccer

momentum
The feeling of going in a positive direction

playoffs
Series of sports games or matches held after the regular season to determine a champion

rivalries
Higher level of competitive fire between teams

tournament
Sporting event featuring multiple teams

venue
Place where an event or series of events is held

Further Reading

Latham, Andrew. *Soccer Smarts for Kids: 60 Skills, Strategies, and Secrets.* Emeryville, CA: Rockridge Press, 2016.

Roth, B. A. *David Beckham: Born to Play.* New York: Grosset and Dunlap, 2007.

Triumph Books. *Soccer Superstars 2017.* Chicago: Triumph Books, 2017.

On the Internet

MLS Next
https://www.mlssoccer.com/next
This website details the future of Major League Soccer.

D.C. United
https://www.dcunited.com/
This official D.C. United site features photos, team news, and statistics.

Best of Jaime Moreno
www.mlssoccer.com/post/2017/01/19/dc-united-legend-jaime-morenos-best-goals-and-highlights-mls
Visitors to this website can watch the highlights of the greatest player in D.C. United history.

Index

Audi Field 13
Beckham, David 27
Boswell, Bobby 20
Campos, Jorge 18
Carreiro da Silva, Fred 23
Center-backs 14
Champions' Cup 20
CR Vasco da Gama 11
Defender of the Year 20
Defenders 14
De Rosario, Dwayne 19, 20, 23
Donovan, Landon 13
Eastern Conference 6, 16, 17
Emilio, Luciano 19, 20, 27
Eskandarian, Alecko 22
Etcheverry, Marco 19, 27
FIFA 4-5
Fullbacks 14
Garlick, Scott 20
Goalkeepers 14
Goalkeeper of the Year 20
Golden Boot 20
Gomez, Christian 19, 27
Hamid, Bill 20, 23
Headers 15
InterAmerican Cup 11
L.A. Galaxy 8, 16, 22, 27
Lassiter, Roy 20
Major League Baseball 13
Major League Soccer 5, 6, 7, 8, 11
Manchester United 13
Medved, Shawn 20
Midfielders 14, 15
MLS Cup 7, 17, 22
Moreno, Jaime 19, 20
National Football League 13
Neal, Lewis 23
Olsen, Ben 22
Open Cup 23
Perkins, Tony 20
Playoffs 7, 10
Pope, Eddie 18, 20
Portland Timbers 7
RFK 11, 12, 13, 21
San Jose Clash 8
Sannah, Tony 20
Seattle Sounders 5, 16
Soros, George 13
Spartan Stadium 8
Supporters' Shield 23
Talon 16
United Soccer League 11
U.S. Open Cup 11, 23
Western Conference 6
West Ham United 23
Wingbacks 14
World Cup 4

About the Author

Marty Gitlin is the author of more than 150 books, mostly about sports. He won more than 45 awards during his 11 years as a newspaper sportswriter, including a first place for general excellence from the Associated Press. That organization also selected him as one of the top four feature writers in Ohio in 2002. Marty lives with his wife and three kids in Cleveland, Ohio.